TEN
MONDAYS
for
LOTS OF BOXES

by

SUE ANN ALDERSON

Drawings by

CADDIE T'KENYE

RONSDALE PRESS
1995

RONSDALE PRESS
3350 West 21st Avenue
Vancouver, B.C. Canada
V6S 1G7

Typesetting: The Typeworks, Vancouver, B.C.
Printing: Hignell Printing, Winnipeg, Manitoba
Cover Design: Cecilia Jang
Cover Art: Caddie T'Kenye
Set in Bembo, 14 pt on 20

The publisher wishes to thank the Canada Council and the British Columbia
Cultural Services Branch for their financial assistance.

Canadian Cataloguing in Publication Data

Alderson, Sue Ann, 1940–
Ten Mondays for lots of boxes

ISBN 0-921870-32-9

I. T'Kenye, Caddie.   II. Title.
PS8551.L44T46   1995   jC813'.54   C94-910867-7
PZ8.3.A3617Te   1995

CAST OF CHARACTERS:

Lots of Boxes—a boy

Lots of Boxes' Mum—a mum

Easy as Pie—a boy

Sky Climber—a girl

The Wandering Blue-Eyed Glumfy—a dog

Thundering Dunderblusses—a herd of busses

The Thronk—a thronk

ON THE FIRST MONDAY,

the hard part was:
Lots of Boxes and his Mum had to move right across town,
had to move from the big old house with three apple trees,
had to move to a little old house with twin plum trees.
A good move,
                    a bad move—
                                which move was this move?
Lots of Boxes didn't know.

The good part was: Lots of Boxes knew
how to pack his stack of boxes.
He'd named himself Lots of Boxes because
that's what he liked the best——
castle boxes, fort boxes, ship boxes,
boxes for climbing on and piling up and crawling into. Yes!

"Sweet commotion!" said his mum, tucking him into bed.
"How will we take all those?"
"We'll pack them on the outside of everything
we'll pack on the inside of them," Lots of Boxes said.

ON THE SECOND MONDAY,

Mum said, "Too many, too much of a packrat muchness!
You'll have to part with some."
So Lots of Boxes and his best friend, Easy as Pie,
had an excellent garage sale.

Lots of Boxes put out everything he was finished with:
3 tennis balls, 2 robins' nests with 5 feathers,
9 green marbles, 1 too-small blue cap,
1 wasp's nest, 8 horse-chestnuts,
and the back half of a train.

Easy as Pie put out everything he was finished with:
6 horse-chestnuts, 4 yellow balloons with 7 bits of string,
10 sea shells, 1 too-small red cap,
1 tin of blue playdough, 1 mouse's skull,
and the front half of a train.

"Want to trade?" asked Easy as Pie.
"Yes," said Lots of Boxes, "let's!"

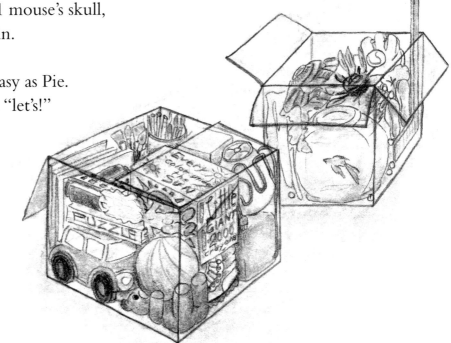

ON THE THIRD MONDAY,

the first thing Lots of Boxes did after he moved
was call up Easy as Pie.
"We're still friends," said Lots of Boxes.
"Now we're telephone friends."
"Always will be," said Easy as Pie.
Lots of Boxes felt better.
Now all he needed was a face-to-face friend,
one with the right sort of name.

He went for a walk on the beach near his house.
He walked out to the edge of the crabbing dock.
A girl was pulling in her crabtrap, hand-over-hand.
Lots of Boxes helped her, hand-over-hand.
At the bottom of the trap, two small brown crabs wrestled.
"Want to toss one back?" asked the girl.
She showed him how, behind the claws, to thumb-and-finger
round the middle. They tossed them back together.

"What's your name?" asked Lots of Boxes.
"Sky Climber," said the girl. It was
the right sort of name.

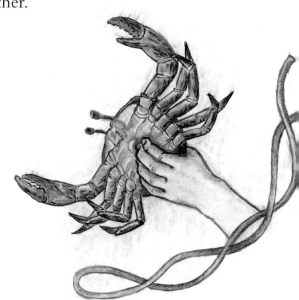

ON THE FOURTH MONDAY,

Lots of Boxes and Sky Climber found
pet racing crabs on the beach
under one black rock or another.
At race time,
they held their crabs gently,
counted one-two-three-go!
and let the crabs go free.

Lots of Boxes' crab skittered to the left,
found a twist of red tree root,
and in its shade, he
stopped.

Sky Climber's crab skippled further, further, further,
but he went exactly
backwards.

"Who won?" asked Lots of Boxes.
Sky Climber said, "Yours
was first to find a tree root. Mine
went backwards faster.
They were running different races:
they both won the one they raced in!"

ON THE FIFTH MONDAY,

Lots of Boxes made a Thronk
from his blue playdough and some sticks.
He set it on the lawn between the plum trees
to see what it would catch.

A Wandering Blue-Eyed Glumfy came.
He shied at the Thronk;
he bellied up to the Thronk;
he sniffed the Thronk all over.

Then the Glumfy wagged his tail
and ever so gently
picked the Thronk up in his mouth.
Squashes galoshes!
How that Wandering Blue-Eyed Glumfy did run CIRCLES on that lawn!
He looked about to take off and FLY
with that zesty Thronk held
ever so gently in his mouth.

When the Glumfy started to look skizzy,
Lots of Boxes clapped his hands,
and the Thronk came right back to him,
bringing the Wandering Blue-Eyed Glumfy with it.

Ever so gently, Lots of Boxes
took the Thronk from the Glumfy's mouth and said,
"Catching a Wandering Blue-Eyed Glumfy
is pretty good for your first time out!"

The Glumfy looked at the Thronk
in Lots of Boxes' hands
with love shining in his blue eyes.
The Thronk looked
                    pleased as peaches.

ON THE SIXTH MONDAY,

when the clouds were full of highjinks,
Lots of Boxes scootered his mum to the library.
At the corner, Lots of Boxes stopped.
A herd of Thundering Dunderblusses
was stampeding wild and reckless.
"Sweet commotion!" said Lots of Boxes' mum,
"we'll never get across!"
"We will," said Lots of Boxes.

Then he held his arm straight up and turned
the flat of his palm to the wild rampaging herd.
And the front row of Thundering Dunderblusses saw
Lots of Boxes stand there and make the sign,
so they slowed and stopped.
The second row of Thundering Dunderblusses
slowed and stopped, so did the third,
until the whole herd was tame as
penguins on an iceberg in mid-summer.

And then, Lots of Boxes scootered his mum
across the street and right through the front door
of the library!

ON THE SEVENTH MONDAY,

Sky Climber planted a strawberry bed.
She watered it and weeded it
and watched the seedlings blossom.
"Thirteen blossoms. Thirteen blossoms in May
means thirteen fresh strawberries in June."
Sky Climber dreamt strawberries.

One night the Wandering Blue-Eyed Glumfy
found the strawberry bed.
"Looks like a soft bed to me," he must have mumbled.
The Glumfy scratched around and churned a round hollow
in the soft rich earth to fit himself
curled-up-and-tail-tucked-in.
The Glumfy dreamt soft, rich earth.

Next day, the Glumfy was gone,
the strawberry seedlings were in shreds,
Sky Climber felt torn inside and mangled.
"Looks like the Glumfy was here," said Lots of Boxes.
"You need a fence."

Sky Climber and Lots of Boxes
built a fence.
They planted more strawberries.
Sky Climber made a sign:
"Glumfy, Keep Out!"

Across the yard, they dug
a new patch of soft, rich earth.
Sky Climber made a sign:
"Glumfy Bed—Glumfy, Sleep Here!"

Lots of Boxes said: "Maybe Glumfys
will grow in the Glumfy bed—
Glumfy sprouts and Glumfy blossoms
and thirteen new Glumfys to pick in June!"

"One Glumfy's enough for me," Sky Climber said.

ON THE EIGHTH MONDAY,

the sky grizzled and drizzled
and the flowers that were already out
drooped and shivered and wanted
to go back in again.

"What we need," said Lots of Boxes, "is a good rainblow."
"You mean a rainbow," said Sky Climber.
Lots of Boxes answered, "No,
I mean a good rain *blow.*"

He opened the window,
put his elbows on the windowsill,
put his chin in his hands,
and blew.
Sky Climber did this too.
They blew and they blew,
for three whole days, until
they'd blown the rain away, every last drop,
and the sun came out.
The flowers stretched and shook themselves.

Over the whole green world
a perfect rainbow arched in the crystal sky.

ON THE NINTH MONDAY,

Easy as Pie rode a Dunderbluss and came
to visit Lots of Boxes and Sky Climber.
They went walking barefoot on the beach.
The Wandering Blue-Eyed Glumfy came too.

Easy as Pie thought the sea smelled like
licorice and oranges
and smoke from a wood fire.

Lots of Boxes thought the sea smelled like
milk and new leather shoes
and plum trees in blossom.

Sky Climber thought the sea smelled like
strawberries and cinnamon
and sardines.

The Wandering Blue-Eyed Glumfy must have thought
the sea smelled like
                            CATS!
because he chased the little waves coming in at him
and running back, further and further out
until the Glumfy was four-feet-up and swimming!

And when he beached, he shook a fine sea shower
all over them, and they played a game of chase and race
on the fine damp sand until they were all four
                                                huffed-out.

Then they plunked flat down
in the middle of their own footprints
to watch cloud-pictures chase and race across the sky.

ON THE TENTH MONDAY,

Lots of Boxes was swinging, toes up high and skyward
on the just right swing
he and Mum had hung on one plum tree.
Sky Climber was building a ladder around the other.
The Thronk and the Glumfy watched.

Lots of Boxes thought about his old house
and the apple trees and Easy as Pie's visit.
Moving away from may be hard,
but *moving to* worked out all right
in just awhile.

A good move,
        a bad move–
                which move was this move?
Lots of Boxes knew. He smiled.